Fix It, Fox

D1475825

WRITTEN BY PATRICIA ANN LYNCH
ILLUSTRATED BY JANE CAMINOS

Pig said, "Fix it, Fox."

Fox put the pot in the box.

Mouse said, "Fix it, Fox."
Fox put the pan in the box.

Cat said, "Fix it, Fox."
Fox put the pen in the box.

Dog said, "Fix it, Fox."

Fox put the fan in the box.

"Fix the pot."
"Fix the pan."
"Fix the pen."
"Fix the fan."

We'll help.

Word Study

box
fix
fox

Can you read these words?

help	it	pan
pot	put	we'll

Stage One
Book 49

DRA	6
Guided Reading	E
Intervention	7
Lexile Level	10
Word Count	62

Modern Curriculum Press

Pearson Learning Group

ISBN 0-8136-0690-0

00001

9 780813 606903